To Trixie,
and her abundant imagination

Printed in Singapore
Reinforced binding

First Edition
10 9 8 7 6 5 4 3 2 1
F850-6835-5-13182

Library of Congress Cataloging-in-Publication Data

Willems, Mo, author, illustrator.
  I'm a frog! / by Mo Willems. — First edition.
     pages cm. — (An Elephant & Piggie book)
  Summary: Piggie introduces his reluctant friend, Gerald the elephant,
to the wonderful world of pretend.
  ISBN 978-1-4231-8305-1
[1. Imagination—Fiction. 2. Friendship—Fiction. 3. Pigs—Fiction. 4.
Elephants—Fiction. 5. Humorous stories.] I. Title. II. Title: I am a frog!
  PZ7.W65535Im 2013
  [E]—dc23   2012034510

Visit www.hyperionbooksforchildren.com
and www.pigeonpresents.com

An ELEPHANT & PIGGIE Book

Hyperion Books for Children
New York
AN IMPRINT OF DISNEY BOOK GROUP

Ribbit!

Piggie?

I was sure
you were a pig.

You look
like a pig.

And your
name *is*
"Piggie."

Ribbit!

I DO NOT TO BE A

It is okay,
Gerald.

No, Gerald. *Pre-tend.*

I am pretending.

Pretending is when you
act like something
you are not.

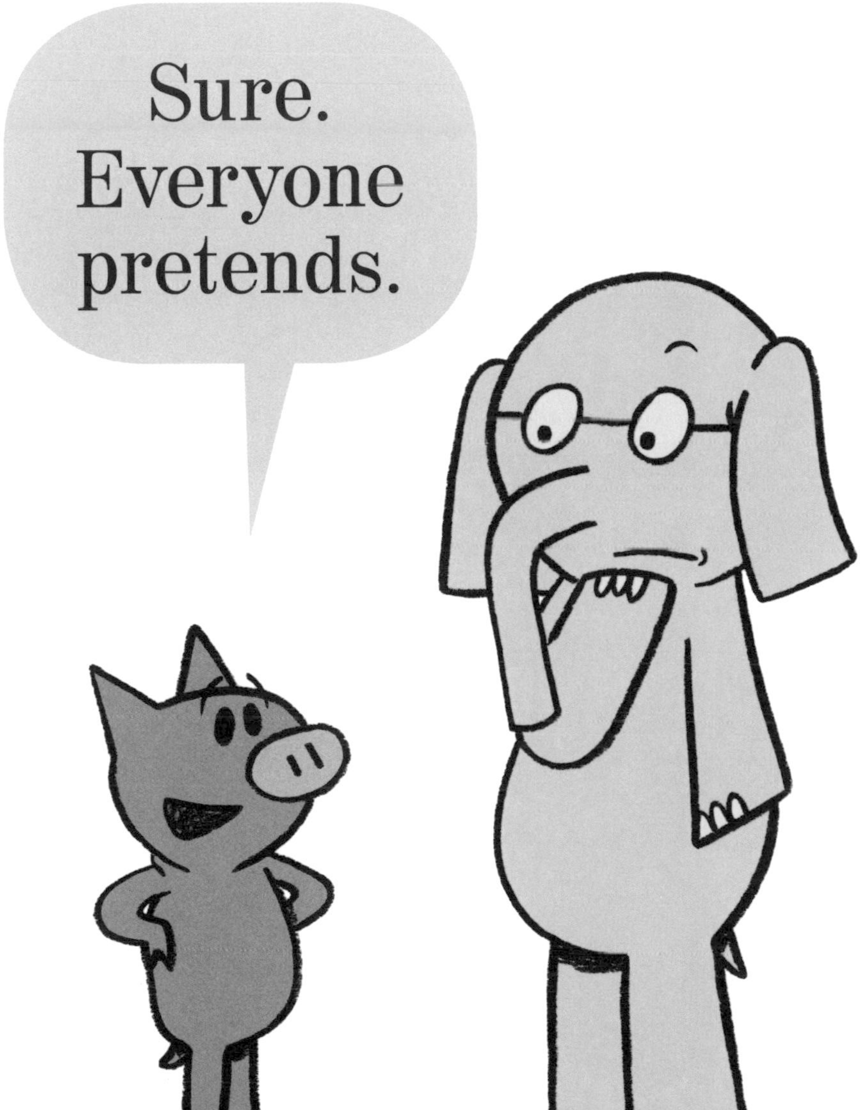
Sure.
Everyone
pretends.

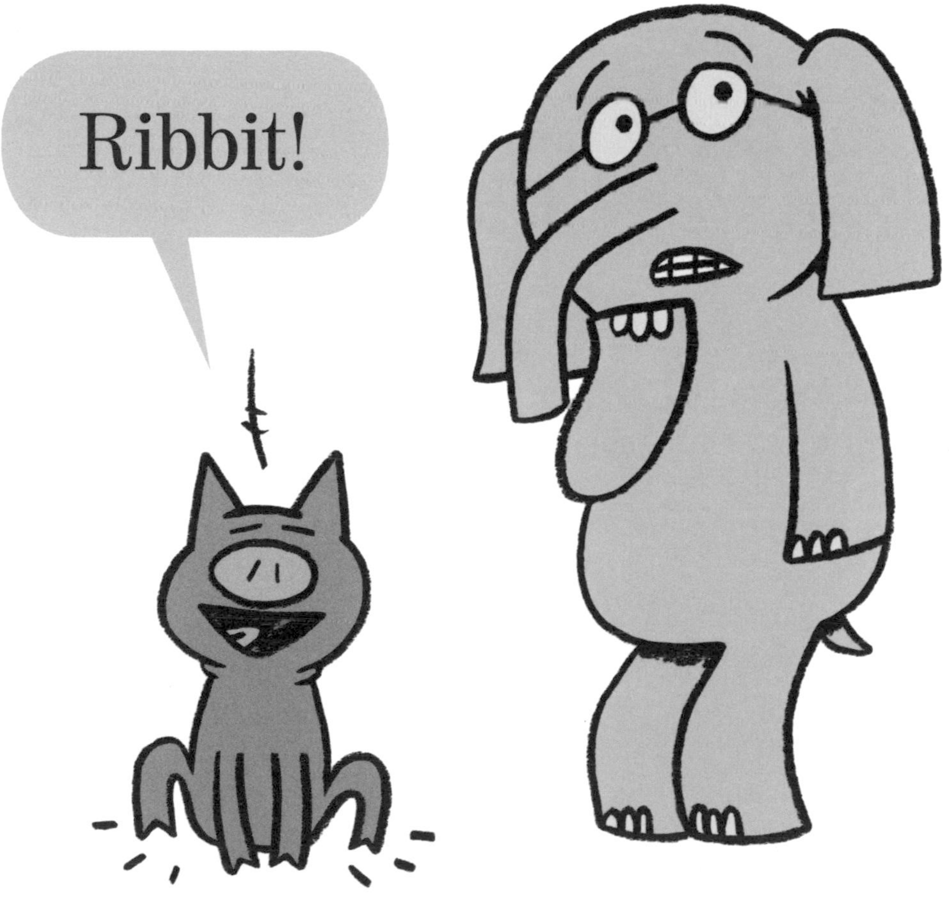
Ribbit!

GERALD!

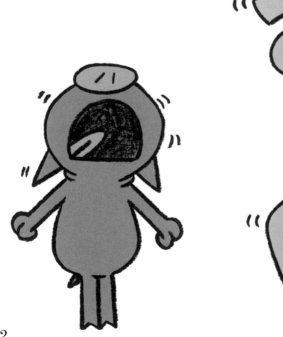

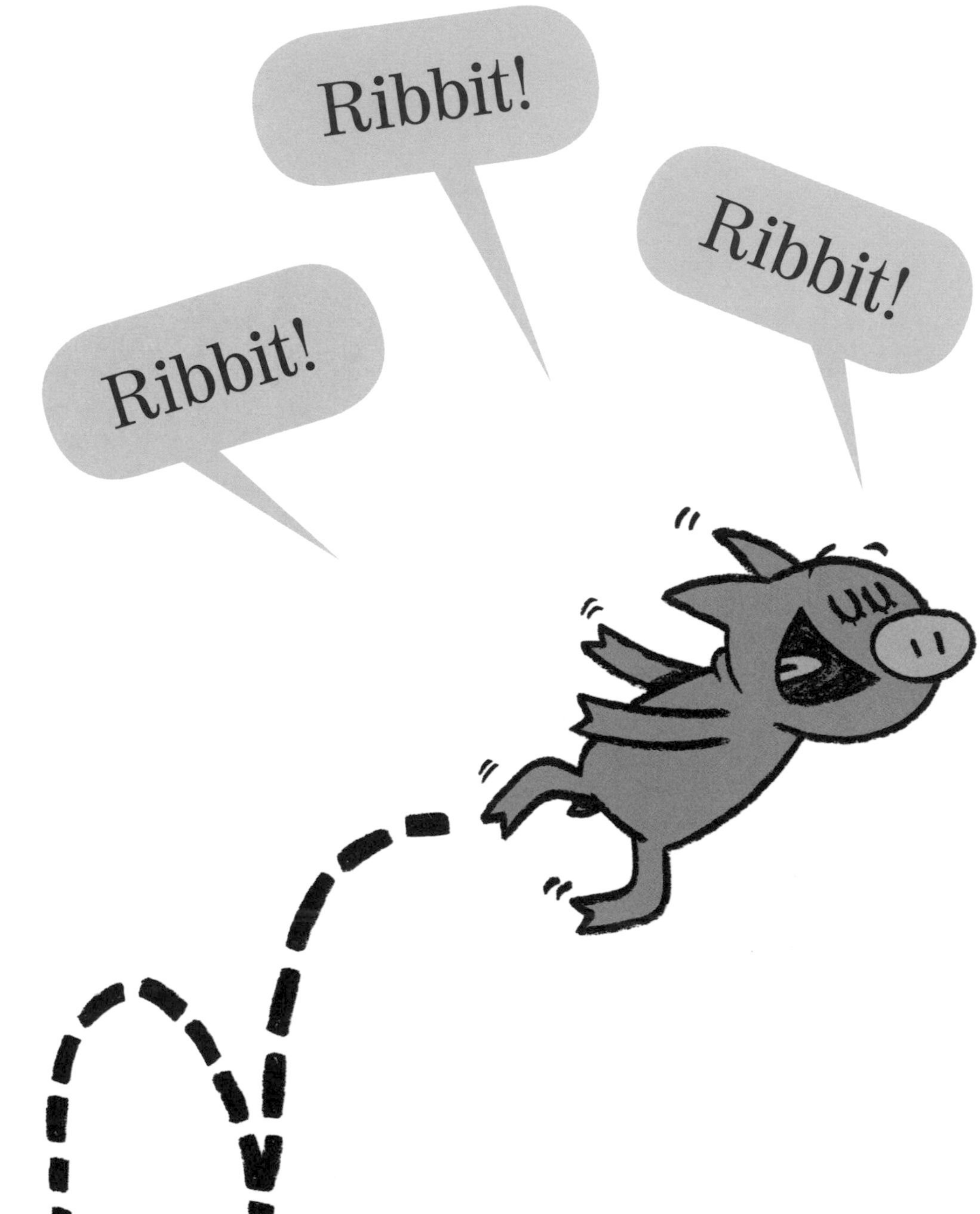
Ribbit!
Ribbit!
Ribbit!

End!

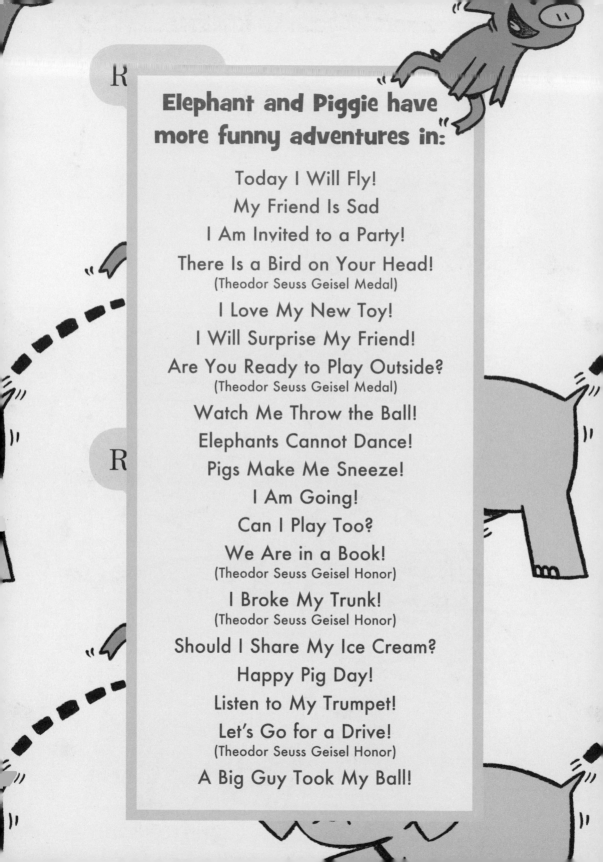

Elephant and Piggie have more funny adventures in: